SAMMY SPIDER'S FIRST SHABBAT

SYLVIA A. ROUSS
illustrated by
KATHERINE JANUS KAHN

KAR-BEN
PUBLISHING

KAR-BEN PUBLISHING
A division of Lerner Publishing Group, Inc.
241 First Avenue North
Minneapolis, MN 55401 U.S.A.
1-800-4KARBEN

Website address: www.karben.com

Library of Congress Cataloging-in-Publication Data

Rouss, Sylvia A.
    Sammy Spider's first Shabbat / Sylvia A. Rouss : illustrated by Katherine Janus Kahn
        p.   cm.
    Summary: Sammy Spider watches longingly as the Shapiro family prepares to
celebrate the Jewish Shabbat, and when the day finally arrives, even he observes
one of its customs.
    ISBN-13: 978–1–58013–007–3 (lib. bdg. : alk. paper)
    ISBN-10: 1–58013–007–0 (lib. bdg. : alk. paper)
    ISBN-13: 978–1–58013–006–6 (pbk. : alk. paper)
    ISBN-10: 1–58013–006–2 (pbk. : alk. paper)
    [1. Sabbath—Fiction. 2. Judaism—Customs and practices—Fiction. 3. Jews—
United States—Fiction. 4. Spiders—Fiction.] I. Kahn, Katherine, ill. II. Title
PZ7.R7622Sap 1997
    [E]—dc21   97–2616

Manufactured in the United States of America
8 9 10 11 12 13 – JR – 13 12 11 10 09 08

A DAY

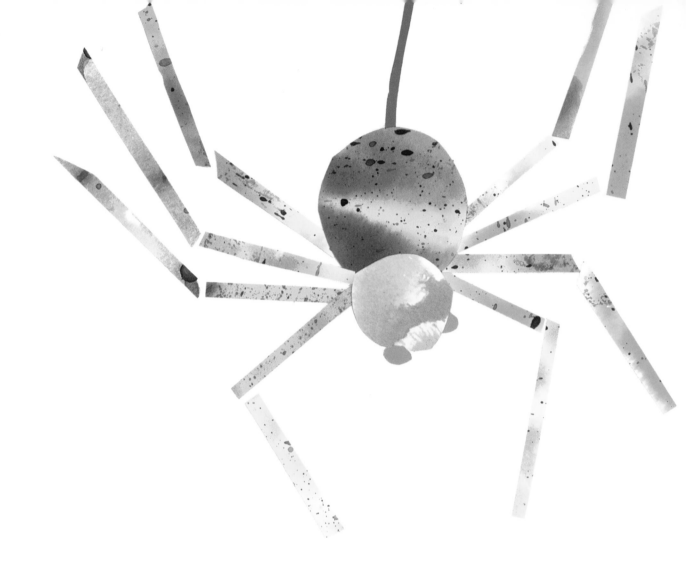

Early Friday morning,
Sammy Spider looked out
the Shapiros' kitchen window.

Josh was turning on the garden hose.
Suddenly a spray of water hit the window
and Sammy jumped back,
snapping a strand of his web.

"Mother!" he called, as he

began

to

fall.

Mrs.

Spider

caught

Sammy

midair.

"What's Josh doing?" Sammy asked, catching his breath.

"He's watering the flower beds," she explained. "Tonight, when the family gathers for Shabbat dinner,

Mrs. Shapiro will put
fresh flowers on the table."

"Will we celebrate Shabbat, too?" Sammy asked.

"Silly little Sammy," answered Mrs. Spider. "Spiders don't celebrate Shabbat. Spiders spin webs. And you need to fix the new hole in ours."

"I'll fix it later," said Sammy.

He was busy watching Mr. Shapiro unpack a bag full of groceries for Shabbat dinner. Sammy looked down at all the food. "I wish I could celebrate Shabbat," he thought.

But when he saw his torn web reflected in the wine bottle, he remembered his mother's words.

"Spiders don't celebrate Shabbat.   Spiders spin webs."

"I'll fix it later," thought Sammy, following Josh into the dining room.

Josh put a bottle of wine on the table. He took out the kiddush cups and candlesticks and put them next to the wine. He put candles into the candlesticks.

The tablecloth reminded Sammy of a huge spider web, and he remembered the hole in his web. "I'll fix it later," he thought.

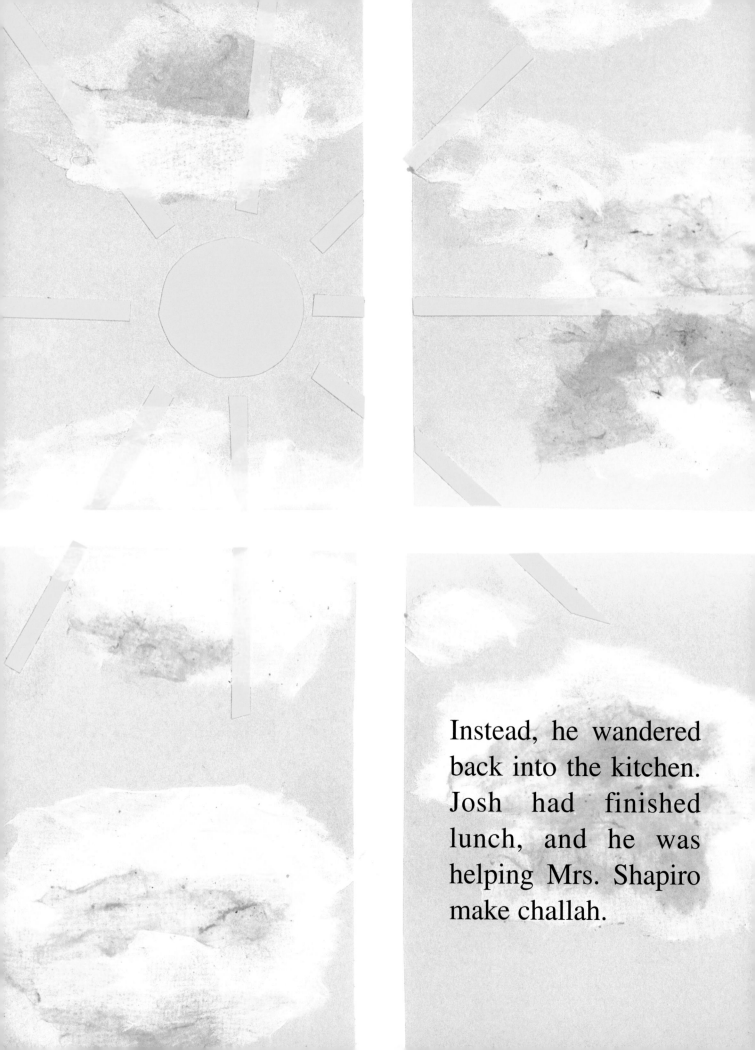

Instead, he wandered back into the kitchen. Josh had finished lunch, and he was helping Mrs. Shapiro make challah.

She kneaded the dough and divided it into three parts. Josh rolled each strip and placed them side by side. Mrs. Shapiro took one strip and crossed it over the middle strip. Then she took another strip and crossed it back over the other way.

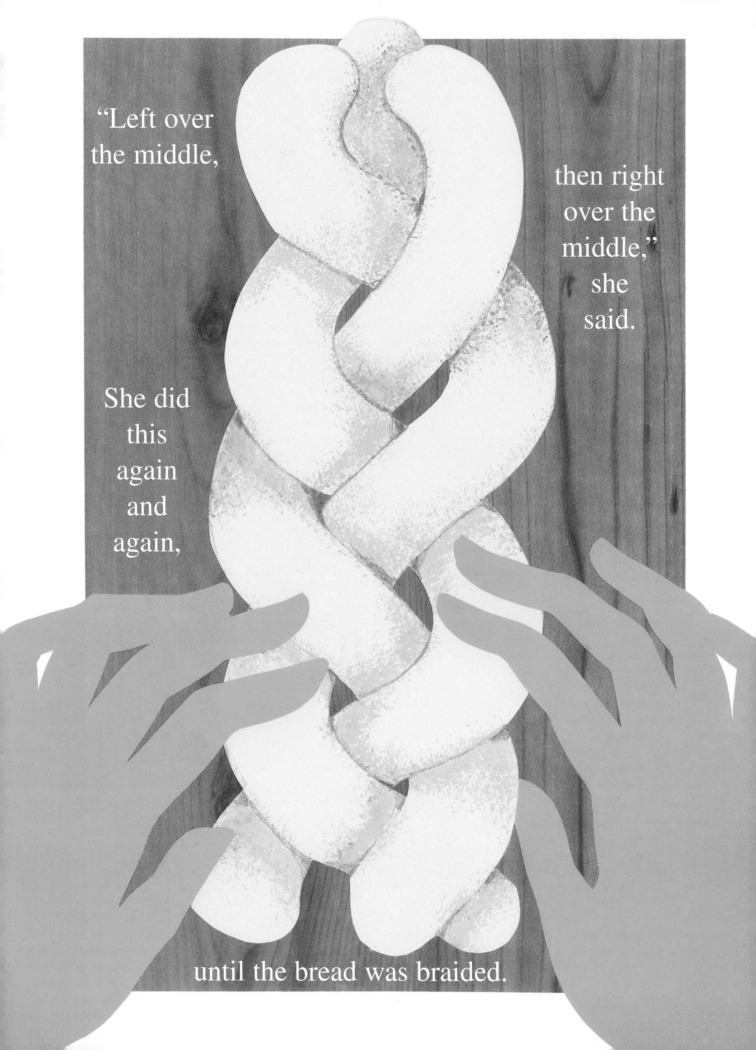

"Left over
the middle,

then right
over the
middle,"
she
said.

She did
this
again
and
again,

until the bread was braided.

Sammy watched carefully.
"Left over the middle,
then right over the middle,"
he repeated,
practicing on the
strands of his web.
The effort
made him tired
and he dozed off.

While Sammy slept,

Josh went up to his bedroom. It was time to clean up his toys.

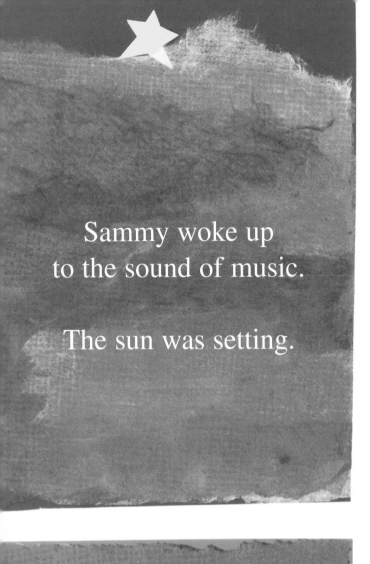

Sammy woke up
to the sound of music.

The sun was setting.

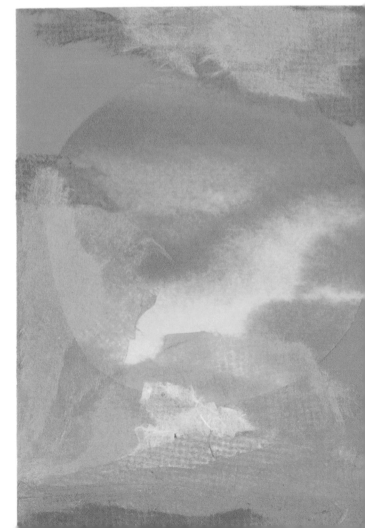

The Shapiros were gathered around the dinner table singing "Shabbat Shalom."

"I wish I could celebrate Shabbat," Sammy thought, as he watched Mrs. Shapiro light the candles and recite the blessing. Everyone sang the blessings over the wine and challah.

Mrs. Spider crawled over
to Sammy and gave him a hug.
"My goodness, you've fixed our web!"
she exclaimed. To his surprise Sammy
saw that the web had been neatly braided
just like a Shabbat challah!

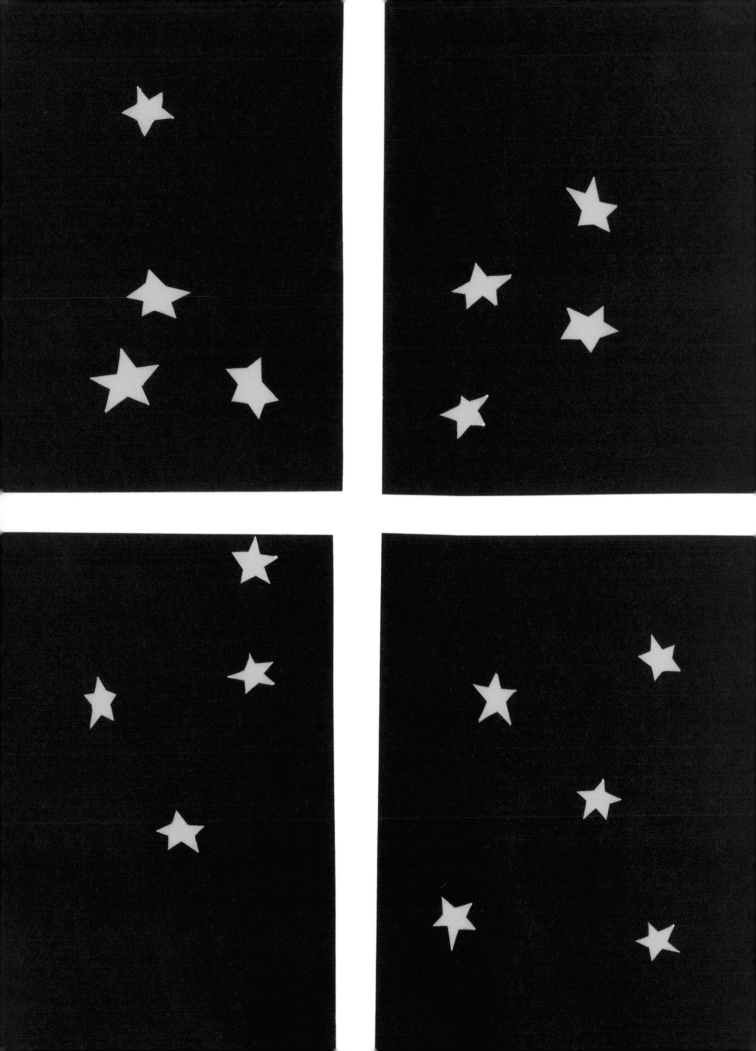

Sammy listened while Mr. Shapiro read Josh a bedtime story. He climbed up his web and fell asleep.

The next morning Sammy watched Josh get dressed for synagogue. He chose his favorite sweater and kippah. When the Shapiros left for Shabbat services, Sammy climbed up his web and noticed a tiny new hole.

"I wish I could celebrate Shabbat," he told his mother. "But I guess I need to fix our web again. I remember how: Left over the middle, right over the middle," he said. "I guess I'll do it now."

"Oh no," smiled Mrs. Spider. "Shabbat is the day of rest. You can fix it later!"

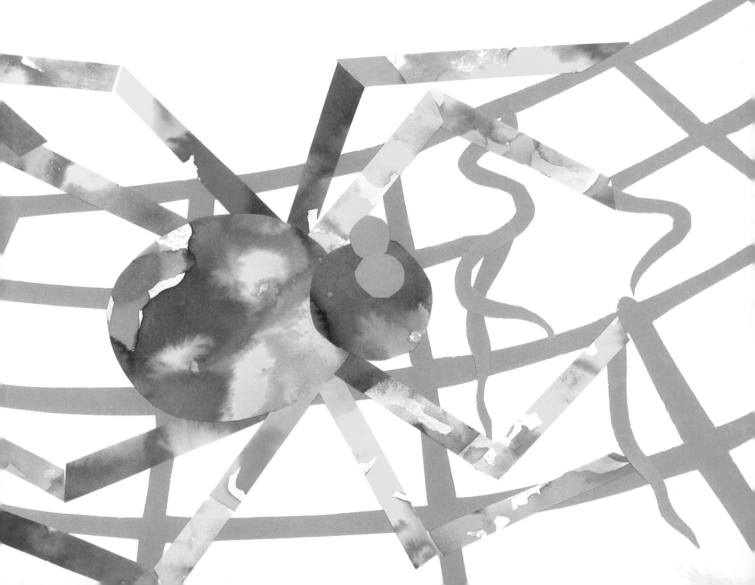

JOSH SHAPIRO'S FAVORITE CHALLAH

(Makes two loaves)

1 package yeast	2 teaspoons salt
2 teaspoons sugar	2 eggs
1 1/4 cup lukewarm water	2 tablespoons oil
4 1/2 cups sifted flour	1 egg yolk (for glaze)

1. Mix yeast, sugar, and 1/4 cup water in small bowl. Let stand for 5 minutes.

2. Sift flour and salt in another bowl. Add eggs, oil, remaining water, and yeast mixture. Mix and form into a ball. Knead on floured board until smooth.

3. Place in bowl. Brush top with oil. Cover with towel and let rise for one hour.

4. Punch dough down, cover, and let rise until twice the size (about 45 minutes).

5. Cut dough in half. Cut each half into three equal parts. Roll into strips and braid.

6. Place loaves on baking sheet, cover, and let rise to twice the size (about 45 minutes).

7. Brush with beaten egg yolk. Bake at 375° for 45 minutes or until golden brown.

TO BRAID: Pinch ends of three strips together and braid as shown. Pinch bottom ends.

CHALLAH BLESSING

The word *challah* means dough. During the time of the Holy Temple, it was a *mitzvah* to give a portion of bread dough to the priests as a gift. Today we fulfill that mitzvah by taking a small piece of dough, reciting a blessing, and burning it in the oven. The blessing is as follows:

בָּרוּךְ אַתָּה יְיָ אֱלֹהֵינוּ מֶלֶךְ הָעוֹלָם, אֲשֶׁר קִדְּשָׁנוּ בְּמִצְוֹתָיו וְצִוָּנוּ לְהַפְרִישׁ חַלָה.

Baruch Atah Adonai Eloheinu Melech ha'olam, asher kid'shanu b'mitzvotav v'tzivanu l'hafrish challah.
Blessed are You, Adonai, for the mitzvah of separating the challah.

BLESSING OVER BREAD

בָּרוּךְ אַתָּה יְיָ אֱלֹהֵינוּ מֶלֶךְ הָעוֹלָם, הַמּוֹצִיא לֶחֶם מִן הָאָרֶץ.

Baruch Atah Adonai Eloheinu Melech ha'olam, hamotzi lechem min ha'aretz.
Blessed are You, Adonai, for the blessing of bread which we will now share.